The Little Pirate Queen

A smooth sea never made a skilled sailor
– Franklin D. Roosevelt

First published in the UK in 2021
by New Frontier Publishing Europe Ltd.
Uncommon, 126 New King's Road, London, SW6 4LZ
www.newfrontierpublishing.co.uk

A CIP catalogue record for this book is available from the British Library.

ISBN: 978-1-912858-98-9
Edited by Stephanie Stahl • Designed by Verity Clark
Printed and bound in China
1 3 5 7 9 10 8 6 4 2

The Little Pirate Queen

Sally Anne Garland

NEW FRONTIER PUBLISHING

Every week, Lucy sailed across the sea on her rickety raft trying to find Far Away Island. Nobody had ever reached its silver shores before or knew what treasure it held.

Her small, creaky raft
had been through
some rough seas lately
and it constantly
needed to be mended.

Although she sometimes
struggled to patch holes,

tie things down,

and mend the sail,

she became quite
good at sailing.

Other children seemed to race past easily in their little boats, and Lucy wished she had a shiny new yacht,

a fast speedboat,

a sturdy rowing boat,

or even just a bouncy dinghy like the others had.

Sometimes she imagined she was a brave Pirate Queen
sailing the high seas, and everything would feel a bit better.

But sometimes, she just didn't feel brave at all.

One morning a wind began to blow.
Then a huge, gigantic wave swept away
Lucy and all the other children
with their boats.

The sky darkened and around her was only stormy water, with no sign of Far Away Island.

Lucy managed to climb back onto her raft, but the sail was in pieces. She was all lost at sea, wondering what to do next.

Suddenly Lucy caught sight of four children further ahead, bobbing up and down in the water. Her little boat was frail, but she rowed frantically to get closer to them. The little girl struggled against the swirling waves.

Lucy helped the children climb safely onto her little raft.

She showed them how to mend the sail, then taught them how to row. Perhaps they would find Far Away Island after all.

Off they struggled against the wind and rain and stormy sea.

After a while, the stormy clouds blew away to reveal twinkling stars. Nighttime had come and the waves now gently lapped at the raft. They huddled together, listening to Lucy's stories of pirates and lost treasure.

In the brightness of the moonlight, she taught them pirate songs too, about silver sands and wild forests filled with adventures.

But by morning, they had all started to feel very tired, and the little boat slowed down with no sign of land in sight. Lucy's songs and stories stopped. Instead there was a silence as even she started to doubt they would ever make it to Far Away Island . . .

Suddenly, she heard something knocking against the little raft.

Lucy looked over the edge of the raft and saw an old, broken mast, with part of its sail still remaining.

It bobbed on the surface of the water, so they managed to heave it on board.

They attached the little sail
to the mast, and hoisted the
two sails high.

Other bits of broken boats were found along the way, and the children gathered them for building. There were parts of decking, thick rope, wooden wheels, large boxes, rudders . . .

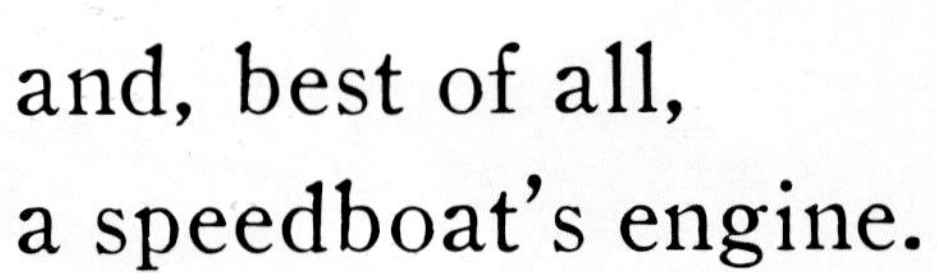

and, best of all,
a speedboat's engine.

With both sails, Lucy's boat swept along. She steered proudly at the helm, for they had all built something truly amazing . . .

a great BIG
pirate ship!

The boat powered through the waves,
scouring the horizon for Far Away Island, until —

'Land ahoy!' Lucy cried—they had found it.
With a hearty cheer, they set a course and sailed
for the island's silver shores.

The ship rested still in the shallow waters of Far Away Island. They all got off, all except Lucy; she had found her sea legs.

'Oo-aar-r-gh, there be treasure on this island!' she shouted at the top of her voice. She watched as the others excitedly ran to find their own adventures on its silver shores and in its wild forests.

Then off she set, the Little Pirate Queen in her wonderful pirate ship, helping those she found lost at sea along the way.